MADG

Based on *The Railway Series* by the Rev. W. Awdry

Illustrations by
Robin Davies

EGMONT

EGMONT

We bring stories to life

First published in Great Britain in 2009
by Egmont UK Limited
239 Kensington High Street, London W8 6SA

Thomas the Tank Engine & Friends™

CREATED BY BRITT ALLCROFT

HiT entertainment

ISBN 978 1 4052 4419 0
1 3 5 7 9 10 8 6 4 2
Printed in Italy

This is a story about Madge, a snub-nosed lorry with three wheels. Madge likes to help the engines on the narrow gauge railway with their work. But sometimes she forgets she has her own jobs to do ...

Up in the mountains, there are many railway tracks that the little narrow gauge engines run on. There are many roads for the cars and lorries, too.

Madge is a snub-nosed lorry. She drives up and down the mountains and valleys, delivering goods to the villages.

Madge is a kind lorry. She likes to take care of everyone she meets, especially the narrow gauge engines.

One morning Mr Percival, The Thin Controller, was telling Madge about a country show and engine rally to be held the next day. Rheneas and Skarloey were going to lead the rally!

"The engines must be clean and shiny. You must take them some soap and brushes," The Thin Controller told Madge.

Madge was pleased. "I'll deliver them right away!" she smiled.

Madge had an important job, too. She was going to pull the brass band at the show so she needed to look her best, as well.

"I'll be the cleanest lorry you have ever seen!" Madge told The Thin Controller.

She honked her horn proudly and set off for the coal mine.

When Madge arrived, Rheneas was very dirty from pulling trucks of coal. The crew took the soap and brushes and began scrubbing him for the engine rally.

Madge stayed to make sure Rheneas was clean and shiny. "Scrub his number and nameplate!" she called. She waited until his whistle was washed and his boiler bands were buffed.

"There! You're almost ready for the rally," Madge smiled. "Just remember to wash behind your buffers!" she called, as she drove away.

Madge had to hurry. She drove faster and faster. But the mountain roads were dirty, and mud splashed her paintwork.

"Oh dear," she thought. "I must get back in plenty of time. I have to be washed, too!"

When Madge steered into the Quarry, Skarloey was also very dirty from his morning's work.

"You're a real mucky buffers!" said Madge. "We'll have to work very hard to get you ready for the rally!"

Soon, Skarloey was covered in soapy bubbles. Madge stayed to watch – she wanted to make sure he would be really shiny!

"Scrub him from funnel to footplate!" Madge told the crew.

It took a long time, but at last Skarloey was clean.

"You'll look grand at the engine rally," she called. "Just one more thing – wash behind your buffers!"

Now Madge really was late, and the mountain roads were long and winding.

Madge raced to the village, down more dirt tracks and dusty roads.

"I hope I can get clean in time!" she worried.

When she reached the square, Rheneas and Skarloey had already arrived. Their paintwork gleamed and their domes glistened.

"You look grand!" smiled The Thin Controller. He was very proud of his little engines.

Then he saw Madge. She was filthy.

The Thin Controller was cross! "Oh dear," he said. "You're very dirty!"

"Don't worry!" said Madge. "I'll go and get washed and brushed right now."

But mud had clogged up Madge's exhaust pipe! Suddenly, with a very loud BANG, Madge backfired . . . and sprayed mud all over Rheneas and Skarloey!

Madge saw the brass band arriving. "Oh no!" she worried. "How will we all get clean in time? And I'm the dirtiest of all!"

"We could help," puffed Skarloey.

"But you're dirty, too!" Madge moaned.

"The band is waiting for you, not us!" chuffed Rheneas.

Madge gasped – she knew she had to be extra clean and shiny to pull the brass band. It was time for her to get clean!

"Make sure you clean her wheel arches!" Rheneas said to the crew.

"And wash her windscreen!" Skarloey chuffed.

Soon, Madge was sparkling! "Thank you," she said. "Now you have to get clean again, too!"

She was about to tell the engines how to get extra clean and extra shiny . . . then she saw what their crews were doing!

They were scrubbing the engines' numbers and nameplates . . . washing whistles, buffing boiler bands and polishing Rheneas and Skarloey from their funnels to their footplates.

"My, what a wonderful job!" laughed Madge.

"We knew what to do because you helped us before," puffed Rheneas, kindly.

Madge smiled. She felt very happy.

Soon it was time for the country show and engine rally to begin.

Madge sparkled and shone as she proudly pulled the brass band.

"You both look wonderful!" Madge called to Rheneas and Skarloey.

The little engines blew their whistles proudly, "Peep! Peep! So do you!"

Madge smiled. But she still wasn't sure whether they had washed behind their buffers!

Two Great Offers for Thomas Fans!

THOMAS & FRIENDS

In every Thomas Story Library book like this one,
you will find a special token. Collect the tokens and claim
exclusive Thomas goodies:

Offer 1

Collect 6 tokens and we'll send you a **poster** and a **bookmark** for only **£1.**
(to cover P&P)

My Thomas Story Library - Collect them all

THOMAS & FRIENDS
Story Library

Thomas books available to buy online at www.egmont.co.uk

Available to buy at www.egmont.co.uk
Look out for 8 NEW Thomas Story Library books in August 2009!

Reply Card for Thomas Goodies!

1 Yes, please send me a **Thomas poster and bookmark.**
I have enclosed **6 tokens plus a £1 coin** to cover P&P. ☐

2 Yes, please send me a **Thomas book bag.**
I have enclosed **12 tokens plus £2** to cover P&P. ☐

Simply fill in your details below and send them to:
Thomas Offers, PO BOX 715, Horsham, RH12 5WG

Fan's Name: ....

Address: ....

....

.... Date of Birth: ....

Email: ....

Name of parent/guardian: ....

Signature of parent/guardian: ....

Please allow 28 days for delivery. Offer is only available while stocks last. We reserve the right
to change the terms of this offer at any time and we offer a 14 day money back guarantee.
This does not affect your statutory rights. Offer applies to UK only. The cost applies to Postage
and Packaging (P&P).

We may occasionally wish to send you information about other Egmont children's books but if
you would rather we didn't please tick here ☐